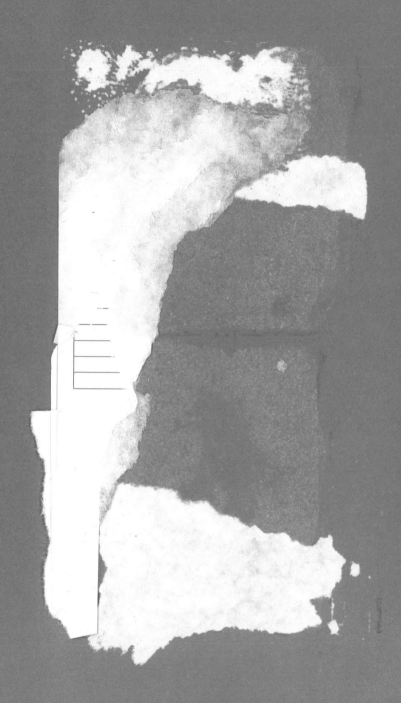

THE Owl WHO
BECAME THE Moon

THE Owl WHO BECAME THE Moon

Jonathan London ▪ Illustrated by Ted Rand

Dutton Children's Books   New York

for Sean, and with gratitude to Karen Lotz J.L.

to my grandson, Theodore Luke Schaller T.R.

Text copyright © 1993 by Jonathan London
Illustrations copyright © 1993 by Ted Rand
All rights reserved.
Published in the United States 1993
by Dutton Children's Books,
a division of Penguin Books USA Inc.
375 Hudson Street, New York, New York 10014

Library of Congress Cataloging-in-Publication Data

London, Jonathan.
The owl who became the moon/by Jonathan London;
illustrated by Ted Rand. —1st ed.
p. cm.
Summary: While riding on a train at night, a young boy listens and
watches as he passes by many creatures in their wilderness homes.
ISBN 0-525-45054-8
[1. Night—Fiction. 2. Railroads—Trains—Fiction. 3. Animals—Fiction.]
I. Rand, Ted, ill. II. Title.
PZ7.L8432Ow 1993 [E]—dc20 92-14699 CIP AC

Designed by Amy Berniker
Printed in Hong Kong
First edition
2 4 6 8 10 9 7 5 3 1

The artist painted the pictures in this book with a traditional
Japanese sumi brush. He used a mixed medium of transparent
watercolors, india ink, and ground chalk; rubbing the chalk
onto one hundred percent rag stock boards to achieve
the graded effects of light and color.

Wouldn't it be nice
to take a ride on a train

through a forest
in the dark
under the stars

when the only sound
is the sound of the train
CHOO-CHOOOO

except for an owl?

WHOO-WHOOOO

While the train climbs
and winds through the forest
around the trees
all covered with snow

CHOO-CHOOOO

the snow flutters
like white butterflies
in the steam
and in the beam
of light
from the locomotive

and the owl soars
silent as a shadow
above the spruce
and ridges of pine

WHOO-WHOOOO

as the cougar searches
down below
with yellow eyes

and the mice and bunnies

scurry and hide.

And the owl
sits on a limb
and winks and *whoo*s
and becomes the moon

As the train
winds down
around a mountain
all covered with snow
the only sound
is the sound of the train

CHOO-CHOOOO

and it ticktacks
down the tracks
and snakes through a tunnel
blacker than night

and across a train trestle
high over a river
hushing
far below.
CHOO-CHOOOO

And the bear
and the cougar curl

in their caves
and go to sleep

and the mice
and bunnies burrow

in their holes
and go to sleep

and the owl
who became the moon
glides
across the sky

on the wings
of a dream.